Princesses of the Pizza Parlor

Ep.1
"Princesses Don't Do Summer School"

By
Maikel Yarimizu

Pizza Master Books
Oklahoma City, Oklahoma

This book is a work of fiction.

All characters, places, and events are works of the
author's imagination. Any resemblance to actual
persons living or dead is purely coincidental.

Cover design and illustration by Astrid Vujnovic

Chapter 1

The Game

Max's Pizza wasn't the biggest restaurant in town, or the busiest, or even the tastiest -- though lots of people said it was anyway. The building had once been a burger joint, and then an ice cream parlor, but Max had done such a number on the place that you'd never know unless you'd lived here all your life. Red-checked cloth covered the tables, and there was a counter along the far end where you could pick up a slice of whatever was available. If you wanted something else, Max was usually happy to oblige.

There were corner booths with deep old sofa seats, leather worn and cracked, and broad tables that were useful for so many things. A lot of business meetings happened here during the week.

However, it was Sunday afternoon right after the lunch rush brought in all the families after church. One table was wiped clean of crumbs and now had all sorts of things gathered upon it.

A white laptop computer, not too old and not too new, sat to the side. A pile of colorful books lay next to it and tons of loose paper. A cardboard box was filled with little figurines, no two alike. And in a big old Mason jar, there were dice, more dice than a kid might think existed. Some were square, with six sides, but more were not. There were little plastic pyramids that counted only to four and others with so many sides that they were almost round. Those counted up to twenty. There was even a blue one that really was round, and it rattled when you shook it.

Helen let the little blue ball fall from her hands and watched it roll across the table. It stopped right in the middle, showing six white dots in two rows.

"If you're gonna mess with the dice, be useful and get them sorted for everyone," her uncle said. He turned back to his conversation. "Thanks again for letting us set up here, Maxine."

"Not a problem. Sunday afternoon and evening are always pretty slow for walk-ins, anyway. And it's Max. You know that." The owner and operator of Max's Pizza had dressed in her usual black slacks, white shirt, and red vest. She looked really smart in it, especially when she stood next to Uncle in his faded jeans and flannel.

The dice came in a crazy rainbow of colors, but it was easy enough to sort them into crowds of sorta-red, kinda-blue, mostly orange, probably purple, and greenish. All the rest -- the clears, the blacks, the metallics, and the whatevers -- she piled up behind the divider screen at Uncle's seat.

"So when are your little friends arriving?" Max picked up a couple of sparkly red dice and rattled them in her fist. "The pies will take a while to cook, after all. Pepperoni still good?"

"And a small supreme for me," said Uncle as he arranged his papers. "Yes, please," Helen said. "Are you sure you don't want to play too?"

"Sweetie, I haven't had the time to sit down for a game in years. I'll just let you and your friends have your fun, and I'll enjoy from the counter."

Helen scooted to her place in the middle of the wide sofa seat and organized her greenish dice in neat lines according to size. First the twenties, then the twelves, the tens, the eights, the sixes, and then her one little four-sided die, a light green with swirls of yellow. She rolled it once, just to see, and it came out with a three on its top point.

"Here's your character sheet, kiddo." Uncle slid the paper over. "Got everything we talked about."

"Thanks, Uncle!"

"Still can't believe your niece talked you into this," said Max.

"What can I say? She saw it on TV, wanted to give it a go, and I'm the only one in the family who knows anything about it. Oh, Helen. Is that one of yours?" He pointed out the window to a blue sedan that had just parked on the side. Two girls were hopping out. One was skinny and taller with a thick mane of orange-brown hair pulled back into a ponytail. The other girl was a full head shorter, with brown pigtails and bangs that almost completely hid her eyes from view. Both of them had enough freckles each to form their own constellations.

"Cynthia! Katelyn!" Helen called and banged on the window until she'd caught the girls' attention. She ran to the door and greeted them with hugs and squeals.

Uncle had resigned himself to a long afternoon, but he put on a good face and shook Mr. McAll's hand. The man had the look of a dad already wishing summer vacation was over, and all he'd done was ferry his daughter and her friend to a playdate.

"Thanks for doin' this," Cynthia's father mumbled through his mustache. "The girls seem t' be lookin' forward to it."

"Yeah, they do. And thanks for chipping in for the pizza and all."

"Worth it, young man. Worth it." And with that, the dad beat a hasty retreat. "So!" Uncle said, turning back to the table. "We're just missing two, right?" "Nope, just one," came a voice from right beside his elbow. Uncle jumped,

tripped, and nearly fell over a roll on the carpet. "Claire!" cried Helen. "When'd you get here?"

"Just now. Rode my bike in." The tiny girl waddled over to the table, then climbed up onto a seat. Her legs didn't quite reach the floor, and her thick, round spectacles barely made it above the table's edge. A single oversized bow stuck out from the back of her head like a pair of floppy rabbit ears.

"Okay then," said Uncle. "Who's missing?"

"Just Shelby," his niece said. She and the other girls piled onto the old sofa seat. "Not sure if she's coming. She wasn't really into the idea."

"I guess we can start then, and she can catch up when she gets here." Uncle picked up a sheaf of paper and tapped it even. Each page had a logo on it, plus a bunch of lines and a whole bunch of numbers. "So, everyone knows what we're up to today?"

"We're gonna have an adventure!" shouted Cynthia. "Gonna tell a story!" Helen added.

"...be princesses," Katelyn mumbled, her eyes darting back and forth a little nervously from behind her bangs.

"More or less all of that. Including the last one." Uncle didn't quite groan at that, but he really wanted to. That had been one of the few things that were completely non-negotiable with his niece. If they were playing a fantasy story game, then there had to be princesses. "So in this game, you each get a character that you have to role-play. She can be just like you or a completely different person. It's your choice, and you'll have some time right here at the start to change things up or choose how she looks.

Anything you want, but," he added with a tap on the paper, "she's completely defined by what's on her sheet here. You can't decide a few hours in that she knows kung-fu or anything, just because it's convenient. So we're going to work on who we are, first of all. Helen, why don't you introduce them to your princess since we already worked her details out?"

"Okay, Uncle! Ahem, my princess is named Gwenevrael, and she's..."

Gwenevrael sat on her favorite branch of her favorite tree in her favorite part of the woods surrounding Lady Amberyll's Academy for Young Ladies. She had her special cloak out, the one her father had given her as a parting gift before she'd left for school, and the magic woven into it made her extra hard to see against the bark.

This came in extra handy when she wanted to hunt, but she wasn't hunting today. Gwenevrael liked to sit here and think sometimes and pretend there was no one else around for miles but rabbits and squirrels and deer and hawks. Sometimes her lightly pointed ears caught the sound of a deer passing by. Sometimes she'd imagine it was a unicorn, even though she knew better.

Eventually, she grew tired of hiding and flipped back the hood of her cloak to reveal the pale skin and arrow-tipped ears of her father's family matched with her mother's red hair and freckles. The sky-blue eyes were hers alone.

She jumped to the ground, startling a family of rabbits as she did, and started walking back to the Academy.

"... so her sheet tells us at the top that Gwen here is a half-elf and that she's trained as a ranger."

"That anythin' like a forest ranger?" asked Cynthia.

"Sort of, but with more arrows and magic. Now, these numbers along the top are for things like how strong she is, how fast and smart, stuff like that. Whenever Helen wants her to do something difficult, these are the numbers we'll be checking. For example, she's got a high dexterity -- she's fast and good with her hands," he added quickly. "So, any time she has to do something quick and tricky, she gets a plus-three bonus. With me so far?"

"What's the stuff along the side?" asked Claire. The little girl was standing on her seat to look at the paper better. "Riding, climbing, swimming..."

"Just what it looks like," said Uncle. "Those are things that she is or can be good at, with the bonuses based on the numbers up top. Now, I've already drawn up a bunch of characters with their base stats and skills assigned, so we could get things started faster. What kind of princess would you like to be?"

"Like Snow White!" hollered Cynthia. "Y'know, singin' and happy and gettin' animals to like her and all."

"Druid princess it is! That means you get to use nature magic, and you have an animal companion," he explained as he handed her the paper. "And for you other young ladies?"

"...um.. could... could I..." Katelyn mumbled. "Can witches be princesses?"

"She's always a witch. Every Halloween." Helen rolled her eyes, and Katelyn's blush spread out from under those brown bangs.

"Nothing wrong with that. And yes, I've got a witch princess in here. Glad I drew some from outside the core classes now. Here you are." He passed the sheet over. "Okay, how about you, Clai--"

"I am the moon princess, here to fight for love and justice and happiness and the future of the Moon Kingdom!" The girl stood on her tiptoes and brandished a plastic wand with a red crystal held in a crescent moon shape. "And I'm tall and beautiful and strong, and all the evil monsters of the dark dimensions shall fear me!"

"Tall?" snorted Cynthia.

"Now, now, I already said that your princess does not have to be just like you.

So, Claire. I take it you like those Japanese cartoons?" "Yeah! Wanna know which one's my favorite?"

"I think I can guess," said Uncle. "Let me check what I've got on my laptop..." Tap-tap-click. "Okay, you can be a cleric princess. That means you're a holy girl who gets her magic from a god or goddess. There isn't a Moon Goddess in the setting we're using, but we can always make one up. Okay!" Uncle announced as he pulled a stack of index cards from his bag. "Three of you can use magic, so we need to go over some basics. First, Helen, could you get the bag of flat marbles? Give everyone else three blues each. For the reds, Katelyn and Claire get two, and Cynthia gets one."

"What're these s'posed to be?" the pony-tailed girl asked. "Looks like somethin' from the bottom of a goldfish bowl."

"These are your magic spells," Uncle explained. He picked up a blue. "These are for level one spells, which your characters should know a few of, and the reds are for level two spells, which they know exactly one each. I already filled out the list on the back of your sheet for you, but we can change them up a little if you want."

He showed them the index cards, which all had colored tabs in green, blue, or red. "These have the details of each spell written on them. Green ones are the so-called level zero spells, which do a bunch of useful but boring things like fetching, cleaning, or mending. You get to choose four of these each day, but you can use them any way you want, as much as you want."

Helen took the cards, and the other girls crowded around to check them out. It had taken Uncle most of an afternoon and evening to fill out the necessary information in a way that was clear, and he'd tried to make it funny as well, with descriptions like "Makes a magic snowball that you can stuff in someone's ear, down their pants, wherever. Good for getting people to chill out." He hoped their giggles were for the jokes he'd intended.

This gave him a free moment to check over some details, at least. Silently, he thanked Max for giving him the shop's wi-fi key. Having an internet connection available made things so much easier. "Okay, Claire? Could you come over for a bit?"

"Yes, o inimitable maestro of the grand game of the imagination?"

"... save it for the roleplay, kid." He pulled a chair over so she could see the laptop screen with him. "So a cle... er, holy girl's got to choose some things called domains. It has to do with who they're supposed to be serving. I'm guessing you're okay with the Love and Moon domains?"

"In the name of the Moon, I shall bring peace and love to the world!"

"Right... I'll take that as a yes. Now, as a holy girl --"

"Princess."

"Yes, as a holy princess, you get a few extra tricks connected to your domain. On top of that, I can give your holy scepter a special power based on the Moon..." He scribbled a note and handed it to her to read.

"Um.. does this say I get a light saber?"

"I guess you could call it that. You can only use it a limited amount of time per day," he added. "Based on your character's level."

"Awesome. Um, what level are we starting at? One?"

"Good question. Okay, ladies!" he called for attention. "Seeing as you are all princesses, Helen and I came to some agreements. First, you're all starting at level three, probably because of excellent tutoring options."

"Awesomesauce! Moon Laser Sword Magic!"

"Um, Mr. Man?" Cynthia raised her hand. "How do we get magic back after we use it?"

"That depends. You all need to get a good night's sleep to really recharge, but beyond that, druids need to meditate on nature for a bit. Moon Princesses need to say their prayers every evening. Witches just need a good rest and some quality time with their familiars. Now, have you all cho--"

"NO, NO, NO! I don't wanna, and you can't make me!"

All heads turned toward the front door. There, a tanned, burly man with more blond hair on his face than on his head was all but carrying a girl one-handed into the restaurant.

This was a particularly impressive feat because she was taller than any of the kids at the table by almost a full head and looked like she spent most of her time running around outside and kicking stuff.

"Now, now!" said her father. "You promised your friends you'd be here, and I ain't gonna let you weasel out of it that easily. See? They're already here!"

"Hi, Shelby!" shouted Helen, with the chorus of other girls following a moment
later.

"Hrmph." The girl managed to slouch her way across the room, squeezing onto the couch next to the others.

"I'll be back to pick you up around six, honey!"

"Whatever." Shelby's face was so sour it could be mistaken for lemonade. Curly black hair stuck out in all directions but mostly downward toward the collar of her soccer team t-shirt.

"So, er, Shelby," said Uncle. "Ready to be a princess?"

"No."

"Aw, don't be like that," said Helen. "It's not going to be dresses and balls and stuff. We're going to have adventures!"

"Defend nature!" cried Cynthia. "...do magic stuff."

"Punish evil-doers in the name of the Moon!"

"Anything you want, really," said Uncle. "Helen, how about you go over the options with her? We could use a fighter of some sort in this game."

That perked up Shelby a little. "So I don't gotta be some stupid Disney pretty princess?"

"Well, I made it a house rule that everyone's got the same charisma score, so you're all equally pretty princesses, but..." Uncle shrugged. "It's your show, ladies. I'm just organizing it. If you want to change your characters, customize them a bit, then now is the time."

"C'mon, Shelby. Let's get you a cool battle princess," said Helen. She grabbed the remaining character sheets, as well as a couple of old artbooks that Uncle had brought along.

"Good, good. Now, um, Katelyn? Could you come over?" "...yes?"

"You'll need to speak a little louder, kid. First question, what sort of familiar animal do you want for your witch?"

"... can I have a cat?" "Excuse me?"

"I..." The girl coughed, then raised her voice a little. "Can I have a little black cat with a white spot on his chest?"

"Don't see why not. And kitties give you a bonus on stealth, so..." He checked a few boxes on her character sheet. "You're all set for some sneaky tricks. That okay with you?"

His only answer was a shy smile.

"Okay, now as a witch, you can get some special tricks. I've got the list here somewhere..." He pawed through a ringed notebook for a second. "Yeah, here we are. Hexes. Choose two."

Katelyn squinted through her bangs at the scribbled notes. Uncle's handwriting was, if anything, worse than the fifth-grade average, but he'd tried to keep it readable. Quietly, she picked out two tricks from the list and wrote them on her sheet.

"Interesting selections. This should be fun."

"Can I have these spells, pleeeeeeeeeeeeze?" Cynthia crashed in from the side, shoving a piece of paper in Uncle's face. Her handwriting was about as messy as his, only written larger and with kitty paw prints above the i's and j's.

"Um... Summon Animal, Summon Nature's Allies, Converse with Animals..." He continued reading. "Er, Cynthia, do all of these have to do with animals?"

"Yup!" The girl bounced on her seat, sending her ponytail up and down.

"Okay, some of these are redundant, and a couple are completely out of your ability level. This last one... All-Out Animal Apocalypse isn't a real spell, so no."

"Awww "

"Palaver time!" Uncle called. "Claire, get back over here! We're working on spell lists."

It didn't take that long to sort everything out, though he'd had to put his foot down a few times before they had any sort of agreement. He needed to resign himself to the fact that none of the girls made the sort of decisions he would, but then again, wasn't that the point?

"We're ready!" announced Helen from the other side of the table. She and Shelby had a character sheet in front of them, covered in fresh pencil smudges and eraser boogies.

"Really?" said Uncle. "That was fast. Okay then, tell us what you've got."

Shelby squared her shoulders, picked up the character sheet, and began. "Princess Selvi..."

Princess Selvi, youngest daughter of the Grand Khan of the high plains of Dungivadim, was in the middle of her second practice of the morning. The first had been a warm-up, an easy hour to stretch her arms and legs and listen to the blade of her scimitar sing as it flew through the air. After a half-hour break and a lot of water, she did it all over again, only in full armor this time. Sweat covered her forehead as she cut through the air, but her beloved dragon-scale armor was so wonderful, it moved with her, no problem. Her illustrious father, may his name ever be feared, had given it to her himself before she'd left to attend this stinking school for soft, weak little girls.

Well, she wasn't about to let this place get to her. She was Selvi Khan's- daughter, strong and hot as the desert wind, and she would fight all challengers.

Her practice came to an end in front of a large glass mirror, which was there mainly for the other princesses' dance lessons later in the day. It was bigger and finer than any of the brass mirrors back home, and it was perfect for watching herself move. Taking off her helmet with its horse-hair crest, she shook her own blue-black braids.

She wiped the sweat from her face, dark and dusky like her mother's, but with the greenish color of her honored father's people. A wild grin crossed her face, showing two delicate tusks.

The clan leaders back home looked down on her for her mixed blood, but the girls here feared her for it. Selvi knew which feeling she liked more. One day she would return to the hills of Dungivadim and make sure everyone there felt the same way.

"A half-orc barbarian?" Uncle sounded like he didn't believe what his ears were telling him.

"A half-orc barbarian princess," Shelby corrected. She'd borrowed a hair clip from Helen so that all her curly black hair was pulled back from her face now. "Strong, tough, and plays soccer with the heads of her enemies. You got a problem with that?" The girl stuck out her lower lip and flared her nostrils, daring him to say he did.

"Nope. Anyone else? Helen?" Uncle asked, looking at his niece's character sheet. He knew for a fact that it had 'Enemy of all orcs' written somewhere on it.

"Sounds cool!" "... no problem." "We shall defend the righteous together!" came the chorus from his side of the table.

"Gotta make things interesting. Right, Uncle?" Helen said with a wink.

"Alright then, it sounds like you two have plenty to roleplay over. So!" Uncle continued. "One last thing before our magic-users introduce themselves. I noticed Shelby made special mention of her armor, and earlier on,

Helen's princess had a magic cloak. That stuff's not standard for beginning adventurers. You all are princesses, so I'm allowing you each two heirloom items that are a lot nicer than your characters should have right now. FYI," he added. "If a monster's shooting fire at you, hide behind Princess Selvi."

He opened his ringed notebook to one last list. This one had been decorated in gold pen by Helen the other day and had shiny curlicues all around the edges. "You each have one item already on your sheets, but there's space for one more. Anything on here is okay."

"I picked a magic arrow-holder thing," Helen added. "A quiver."

"Yeah, that was it. Thanks, Uncle. It never runs out of arrows."

Uncle had been more than happy to let her have that one, too. There were already enough things to pay attention to that he didn't want to add keeping track of arrows in a big fight. The rest of the list was eclectic, filled with items that were obviously useful, as well as a few that were just plain silly. As the girls bickered over what to choose, he allowed himself a quick grin.

"Ooh! A lute!" shouted Cynthia, stabbing a finger at the paper. "That's like a guitar, right?"

"Um, sort of."

"Awright! Gonna get that," the pony-tailed girl declared. "And I'm gonna sing all the animals to do what I want 'em to do."

"Er, you do realize your character has no skill points in performance, right?" he asked, while everyone else around the table groaned and shook their heads.

Neither reaction seemed to discourage the girl, if she even noticed at all.

Instead, she sat up in her seat and started to sing: "Oh, since my puppy left me... I've been all over town... " Uncle couldn't tell if what came next was improvised or if there really was a rockabilly song out there about runaway pets, but Cynthia was really belting it out, as enthusiastic as she was off-key.

"Hey, game guy," Claire said once the song was over. "Just call him Uncle," Helen said with a giggle.

"Okay, Uncle game guy! Is this mythril stuff the same magic silver from those movies with the elves and the ring and stuff?"

"Er, yes. It's sometimes called moon silver, too..."

"Perfect! I'm grabbing this Mythril chain vest then. Moon Princess Protection!" The little girl was standing on her seat again, waving her plastic scepter wildly.

Her Holy Highness Princess Cassandrella, the next High Priestess of the Moon Throne of Selunika, stretched her long legs and knelt on her prayer cushion. She was on the dormitory's roof, in a flat little space reserved especially for her because her work was so important. Someone had to greet the Moon every day as it rose over the horizon, which according to her little schedule book, would happen in the late afternoon today. It didn't necessarily have to be her doing it, of course. Her blessed mother was undoubtedly making her prayers right now as well, but every little bit helped.

There! That beautiful half-circle, light of her life, peeked over the mountains to the east. Cassandrella raised her scepter of office, the sign of her service as a priestess of the Moon, and saluted. The sleek Mythril baton was topped by a shimmering crystal caught in a crescent of pale gold.

"I greet thee today, O Bounteous Moon, bringer of light in the darkness, wife of the Sun! To Thee do we cry when misfortune strikes in the night, and from Thee do we gain the strength to strike back. Let me bear Thy light, O Moon, and be Thy righteous blade!"

Pretty much every day, she asked the Moon to accept her service, and every night, the Moon said yes. She could feel the blessings of Her power flowing down, making her holy symbol shine with the light of love.

Princess Cassandrella stood tall and clad in her moon-silk robes and fuzzy bunny slippers; she danced to the light of the Moon in the pale blue sky.

"Claire? Claire!" Uncle was calling. "Earth to Moon Princess, come in!"

Brown eyes opened wide, made even larger by the huge bottle frame lenses on her face. Everyone was staring at her attempts to pirouette on the old sofa seat. Her ankles wobbled, and she fell right onto Shelby.

"Hey! Watch whatcher doin', ya little baby!"

Who're you calling little?" Claire yelled back before she could sit properly. "We're all the same age!"

"Barely." Shelby snorted. "You turned twelve in, what, May? And I'm turning thirteen in August."

"So we're in a three-month window of opportunity? Great!" Uncle declared loudly, clapping his hands. "What will your princess take, Shelby?"

"Whatever."

"Okay then, bone talisman! Carved from a dragon's knuckle," he added. "Perfect for barbarian princesses or heavy metal lovers. Okay, last up is Katelyn. Have you picked anything out yet?"

"...There's no magic broomstick."

"Um, I didn't quite catch that."

"She said there are no magic broomsticks," reported Helen. "Y'know, like for flying."

Uncle shrugged. "Sorry, I wanted to keep the items on the list around the same price, by the game rules. A magic broom of flying would cost at least five times what anything else would be, and your witch's already got a pretty awesome item on her sheet."

"Awww..." said Claire. "Let her have it..." "Yeah, c'mon," chimed in Cynthia.

"It's not that... Look," said Uncle. He shook his head. "This would give her a steed, a flying one, and the rest of you don't even have horses! It's not a good idea for game balance, or... or..."

Five pairs of puppy-dog eyes stared at him from around the table. Katelyn even had her hand pulling her bangs up just to get the effect right. In ragged unison, the girls all cried, "Pleeeeeeeeeeeeeeeeeeeeze?"

"Fine. Fine!" Uncle threw his hands up in the air. "What do I know? I'm just the GM here. Okay! So, Princess... what was her name?"

"... Bianca." "Bianca, Uncle."

"Princess Bianca had a magic broom, a really nice one made of sanded elm wood with a leather seat and everything, only there was an incident a couple of weeks ago involving some silly game with enchanted, weighted balls, and a fellow princess got sent to the infirmary with a concussion, so the broom's currently locked in a closet in the teachers' lounge. Hey," he said to his audience. "I never said I'd make it easy on you all. Now, Cynthia. It's time to introduce your character."

"Awright!" Her reddish ponytail bounced as the girl played air-lute for a moment, then began: "This is the ballad of Flora the Fair...□"

"This is the ballad of Flora the Fair...
With rosy-red cheeks and golden hair...
Like waves of grain upon the plain...
And a voice like birdsong in the air..."

A fingernail caught on a lute string, pulling it with a loud twang and a muffled curse. Princess Flora Fidella Del'Monica sucked her finger until the pain subsided and then started over. Writing a song was harder than it sounded, though. She'd already run out of good rhymes for "fair." Flair? Pair? Pear? Spare?? Nothing really fits.

She sighed. "Got any ideas, Mr. Chitters?"

Up above, from his perch atop Flora's Staff of Plenty, Mr. Chitters the squirrel twitched his red tail and squeaked some advice in a quick burst of clicks and chirps. Squirrel poetry left a lot to be desired, unfortunately. Everything seemed to rhyme with "nuts."

"Welp, it's getting late," she said, noting the sun's place in the sky. "Better be getting back to the Academy."

Mr. Chitters squeaked in protest.

"Yah, yah. I don't like it much either, but at least they let us spend the afternoons out here, right?" In between the school's keep and the outer walls, there was a nice-sized wood that was filled with all sorts of cute and cuddly critters. Only Mr. Chitters ever came back with her to school, though, and that was 'cause he was her special companion. He'd come with her all the way from the forested slopes of Silvalachia and would sometimes complain about the local squirrels' funny accent.

Flora uprooted her Staff of Plenty from where she had planted it in the ground. It'd been her grandfather's, and she was always *amazed at how the roots and branches pulled back into it and became patterns in the carved wood whenever it wasn't planted right. There hadn't been enough time this afternoon for it to grow fruit, though her mouth watered at the thought.*

The druid princess waved to all the other animals, the birds and the rabbits and the deer that had come to hear her sing. Her audience scattered and disappeared into the brush. With a sigh, she turned and headed back to school.

"Not bad, Cynthia." Uncle nodded. "You read the notes on your character sheet, too. Any questions?"

"Is the lute magic, too?" The girl looked like she was about to break out in song again.

"Yes, but I'm not going to tell you how just yet." Uncle winked. "Gotta have some surprises. So let's get this game started for real, shall we? It's the last day of school, and..."

"Uncle!" yelled Helen. "You forgot to let Katelyn introduce her character!"

"What? Oh, sorry about that." He brought his palms together and made a polite sort of bow in her direction. "My apologies. So, tell us about Bianca."

"...Princess Bianca."

Princess Bianca of the Western Winkwoods had buried herself in books. They were piled high on all sides, leaning in precariously but never actually toppling over. She had her own nest of cushions in the heart of the pile where she curled up with a huge tome, an index of magic items. At her side was a large rod, or perhaps a scepter, fancy and ornate with gold wire and gemstone chips. It was a gift from her grandmother, the Witch of the Winkwoods, and it looked quite impressive. She just didn't know what it actually did.

She'd been told that it was up to her to figure it out—one more riddle from Gran'Mama, the old bat. The teachers here at the Academy wouldn't let her test it out directly, not until she knew what it was supposed to do. So ever since they impounded her broom over that stupid ball game accident, she'd stuck to the library with its huge selection of magical encyclopediae and indices. The answer had to be in there somewhere!

Her hat, big and floppy brimmed like a witch's should be, was scrunched up between a set of bookends. Her familiar uncurled his body from around the pointy end and meowed softly. Jinkies was a cute little black cat with a white star on his chest and a huge appetite hiding behind it. He considered it his duty to make sure she was alerted to all mealtimes promptly and with great protest.

"Mrrow! Mrrgl?" Jinkies hopped up on her shoulder and began licking her ear.

"Okay, okay! I'll take a break for lunch!" She placed her bookmark carefully, set the index to the side, and picked up her hat and scepter. "Come along, Jinkies."

The little cat took his customary place around her collar as she left her fortress of solitude and study. The way the books were stacked, there was no way to go but up, which didn't trouble her at all. Bianca ran a hand through her black hair, picking out the single lock of pure white that hung down the front of her face. Her grandmother had taught her a trick – a way to focus a bit of her magic through that lock of hair and make it stretch, extend, and reach up, up, up out of the pile. The rest of her followed right after, pulled up by that magic hair.

She held on to her treasure tightly. It was a mystery and a challenge, and she wouldn't stop until she knew the answer. She would succeed. She knew she would!

"... And I'll find out what it does! For real!..." Katelyn's voice tapered off as she realized she'd just been shouting at the table. Then Uncle began clapping, and a blush flared across her face like a wildfire. She sat back down and tried to disappear into the crevices of the sofa seat.

"No, no, no! That was good!" cried Helen, pulling the other girl back up. "That it was," Uncle agreed. "Good to hear your voice, kid."

The blush didn't fade, but it was joined by the girl's shy smile.

"Breadsticks coming through!" Max swooped in with a basket of appetizers. "You all were looking a little hungry over here. When's a good time to get the pizzas ready?"

"In about an hour?" Uncle suggested. "We're about to take the princesses out for a test drive. Girls! Get your drinks now, or be thirsty for a while longer. Your choice."

The pizza parlor had a self-service drink counter by the register, and while the young ladies were debating the selection, he took the opportunity to re-order the table. When they returned with their drinks and his requested root beer, it was to find a laminated map of a castle that — in this particular game — was known as Lady Amberyll's Academy for Young Ladies. The last time he'd pulled it out of storage, it had been the lair of an undead king, but with a bit of dry erase marker and some new sticky labels, it had quickly been transformed. Around the map, each girl's character sheet was neatly placed along with whatever reference cards and magic counters were needed.

In the center of the map were six figurines. Five had once been chess pawns, but they'd gotten a paint job and a sort of promotion somewhere along the way. The sixth figure was very much still a queen.

"There'll be a little color sticker on the corner of your sheet," said Uncle. "Your princess is a matching color. So on to business! It's the last day of school for the summer, and all the princesses are packed and ready to go through the magic Wayhouse doors to their homelands. You ladies are in the last group to go, but before you can leave, the headmistress summons you to her office."

Lady Amberyll's office was lofty and classically decorated, much like its mistress. Even when seated in her chair, she towered over the five girls. Her hair was silver, but otherwise, she did not look old at all. Sharp green eyes watched the princesses as they filed in, and the ghost of a smile slid across her face.

"Good morning, children," she said.

"Good morning, milady," they responded in chorus, though Princess Selvi rolled her eyes as she joined in.

"Now, I know you must all be busy with the end of the school year," Lady Amberyll continued. "But I have some unfortunate news. The five of you all pass through the Alford Point Wayhouse on the way to your respective realms every holiday, but unfortunately, that house was attacked just last night. Stone giants, you know, very messy things. The magic door was completely knocked to pieces, I'm afraid."

She paused for a moment, watching as they digested this bit of news. The young half-elf caught on the quickest, raising her hand politely.

"Yes, Gwenevrael?"

"What, or rather, how does this affect our travel plans?"

"It rather ruins them. While it may be possible to arrange passage through other Wayhouses, there would by necessity be some long overland trips between them. None of you would likely reach home before it was time to turn around and return here. We are preparing message spells to inform your respective courts of the issue and that you are free to stay on school grounds for the summer."

The young ladies all reacted to that, though some more than others. Gwenevrael simply frowned and looked sad, while Bianca seemed almost happy. Flora and Cassandrella were on the verge of tears, but dear, sweet Selvi...

"This stinks like camel slop!"

... was her usual, charming self.

"Language, Selvi," Lady Amberyll tutted. "Now, I know this is a bit sudden, but at least you're not alone. I'm sure the five of you will find something in common."

The headmistress did have to admit that was something of a long-shot, though. Already the half-elf was glaring daggers at the khan's daughter, with young Cassandrella sitting uneasily between them. The three were as mismatched a set as any she'd seen, with the ranger's greens, the barbarian's dark red and black, and the moon princess's shimmery white raiment all together like that. And then there was Flora on the far left, in homespun cotton and simple leather, not looking a bit like a lady of high birth. On the far right, Bianca had her usual black gown on, as well as that ridiculously large hat she insisted on wearing everywhere.

And then the young witch's cat, who'd spent the last few minutes quietly stalking the druid's squirrel, chose that moment to pounce.

"Mrrowl!" "Squeak!" "Mr. Chitters!" "Hey! Watch where you're—" "Get off me!" "In the name of the Moon--!" "If you touch Jinkies, I'll…"

"Enough!" Lady Amberyll roared, forcing all five girls and two pets into silence. "Like it or not, the five of you will be stuck together for the rest of the summer." The headmistress nailed each of them in turn with her sternest glare. "I understand how disappointed you all must be, but you need to live with it. Now, I suggest that the five of you retire to the parlor on your floor and get to know each other better.

Perhaps plan what you would like to do for the holidays."

A moment later, and they were standing in the cool stone hall of the Academy, with the headmistress's door clicking shut behind them. Ten minutes later, they were sitting around a table in the parlor, just as Lady Amberyll had commanded.

Flora was handing out cups of her favorite herbal tea, the one made with raspberries. Only Selvi turned down the offer. The barbarian princess was slouching back in an overstuffed armchair. Across the table from her, Gwenevrael was carefully cleaning her knives but accepted her cup with one thin-gloved hand. Bianca was sitting on the rug, her cat perched atop her shoulder.

Cassandrella was running into the room with her hands full of clean bed sheets. "What are you going on about?" Selvi growled.

"I heard this in a story! You cut the linens into strips and make a rope so you can climb down from your bedroom window and escape!"

"We're not confined to our rooms," Gwenevrael pointed out. The ranger princess aimed a thumb at her pack, laid out on the floor beside her. "And some of us actually have rope."

"Oh..." The cleric dumped the linens on the floor, then sat on them with a whoomph. "Oh! We could make a big balloon out of them and fly right over the walls!

Bianca could pull us with her broom!"

Uncle scribbled a quick note and passed it over to Katelyn. "... oh."

"What does it say?" asked Helen.

"Flying's not such a good idea," Bianca said, hugging Jinkies. "I tried to fly over the walls once. The gargoyles almost ate me." She shivered at the memory and squeezed tightly. The little black cat rolled his eyes and mewled.

"Where would we even go?" asked Flora?

"Anywhere but here," Selvi said. "Spent enough time here as it is. Ain't staying any longer."

"Let's go to the Moon!" Everyone ignored Cassandrella this time.

"Has anyone even been out the main gates before?" asked Bianca. The other girls shook their heads. Like all the princesses at the school, they'd always arrived by Wayhouse and left the same way.

"Surely one of us knows where we could go!"

"Okay, time out," said Uncle. "This is the perfect opportunity for a knowledge check. The idea is that just because you don't know something doesn't mean your princess doesn't know it if you get my drift. So, for example, Gwen's got a skill point in knowledge of geography. With her other scores and everything, she's got a good chance of knowing where to go. Ready, Helen?"

His niece grinned and picked up her big green die, the one with numbers up to twenty.

"So, the difficulty here is fifteen for full knowledge, but you've got a bonus of seven already. Eight or higher gets it."

The little lump of green plastic rolled from her fingertips, landing on the tabletop and bouncing once, twice, three times. Gatta-gatta-gatta... The die came up with a 3. Helen stared at the number for a moment, then looked to her uncle with a confused face. "Um, what do we do now?" she asked.

"We roll with it. Here's what a total of ten gets you..."

Chapter 2

The escape

"The Academy's out in the middle of nowhere on purpose," Gwenevrael said with a sigh. "That's why everyone uses the Wayhouses to get here. I'm not even sure where we'd be on a map."

"So why don't we find one? A map, I mean." Everyone turned to look at Bianca, still sitting cross-legged on the soft carpet. "We've got a library over in the next building, and it's not like they said we couldn't use it for study purposes. "

But will the librarian let us see the right books?" asked Selvi. "She never lets me touch anything."

"Probably she was convinced you'd rip all the pages," snorted Gwenevrael. "I prefer ripping ears. Pointy ones make for good handholds, too."

"May the Moon bring peace!" shouted Cassandrella, pushing herself between them. "We'll be stuck here all summer at this rate unless we can work together at least a little bit! Now let's have a hug..." That got the cleric two sets of glares. "Um, a handshake?"

Selvi didn't back down, but she didn't push forward either. Folding her arms against her chest, she said, "Okay, until we get out of here, we work together. No longer'n that."

"Agreed." The half-elf sneered.

The school library was a single room, though that word hardly did it justice. It was slightly better to say that it had no walls, only shelf after shelf of books that meandered around the open space like a children's game of dominoes. All it would take was one push, and the whole series would come tumbling down. From the look of things, this may have happened in the past, on more than one occasion.

"You! What mean you here?" the librarian's voice thundered from on high. It was rumored among the student body that Mistress Heyerwif was half-giant by birth, and the woman was, in fact, taller than anyone else in the school. There was an entire series of shelves set into the ceiling, which only she could reach properly. Long blonde hair was pulled back into a bun, and icy blue eyes pinned the gaggle of princesses in place. "Should be home, all of you!"

"Um, our apologies, ma'am," Cassandrella said nervously. "We, we aren't going home this summer. A problem with the Wayhouses..."

"And we've already got extra work to do!" Bianca complained loudly. "Can you believe it? We have to do an in-depth report on the school. Like, twenty or thirty pages each!"

"Ja, ja, that sounds like milady.." Mistress Heyerwif was nodding, and some of the disapproval had vanished from her eyes. "Und so you are needing books, ja?

Anyt'ing pertaining to the school?"

"Yes, please," the five princesses said, more or less as a group. Selvi was scowling at the mere mention of more schoolwork.

"Um, we're all taking different topics for it," said Bianca. "History, famous students, geography, local animals, architecture, whatever there is."

"Hm. Let us see what we can find, ja?" The librarian closed her eyes and whispered the words to a spell. Her fingers twisted and turned in complicated patterns, and suddenly tiny blue balls of light danced between them. Mistress Heyerwif cast the lights into the air, and away they went. "Follow the guides," she commanded. "They will find the books you seek."

The princesses babbled their thanks and rushed off. The tall, blonde woman chuckled as they went.

"Okay, here we are," Gwenevrael said, pointing to a spot on the map.

"You sure?" Selvi didn't sound too certain herself. The old chart was a complicated work of art, but it looked like it valued that artistry over accuracy. The section the ranger princess had pointed out included a fanciful picture of a dragon, for one thing.

"Pretty sure. Here's that mountain to the west, the one with two peaks that you can see from the higher towers. The shape's pretty distinctive."

"So, where does that put us?" asked Flora. She was leafing through a book of animals common to the region.

"About a hundred miles north of the nearest big city." "Pft, that's nothing." Selvi snorted at the thought.

"It's not us that I am worried about." Gwenevrael nodded to the witch and the cleric, who were curled up on the rug, napping. Jinkies was draped under Bianca's chin like a fuzzy neck warmer.

"Hey! Sleeping beauties! Wake up!" yelled the half-orc. Selvi stomped her feet as hard as she could, rousing such a noise that the two girls and the little cat all jumped straight up in the air.

"That was mean," said Gwenevrael.

"Don't say you weren't thinkin' about it," the barbarian countered. "I can tell you're wantin' to smile."

"Am not!"

"So, um." Bianca yawned. "Where's the fire? Have we figured out where we're going yet?"

"The city of Himmel's Gate. Or maybe Gote. Goat?" Selvi scratched her head. "Am I the only one havin' trouble readin' this thing?"

"It is a bit old-fashioned," Gwenevrael acknowledged. "But it's the best we've got. Going to be a long walk," she warned.

"Oh, that's all right. I've got my broom."

"Thought that was locked up in the teachers' lounge," said Cassandrella, who was still rubbing the moon-dust of sleep from her eyes.

"Yup, which is why you're going to help me get it out!"

"I'm going to do what now?" The cleric shook the last of the fog from her head. "No! That's stealing! As the princess of the Moon, I must fight for Truth and Justice, not Petty Larceny!"

"Aww... but it's not stealing," said Bianca. "It's mine, and I'm just, er, liberating it. Then we can use it instead of our feet so that we won't slow everyone else down as much." The witch hooked her arm around Cassandrella's shoulder and made soaring motions with her free hand. "Just think, flying gently through the night, under the light of a big, full moon. "

The cleric's eyes were much like the moon at that thought, big and round and shiny. "Ooooooooooh. "

"So the two of you should go do that," said Gwenevrael. "The rest of us will scout the walls to see where we should sneak out. Meet us by the old oak tree in an hour, okay?"

"In the name of the Moon, we shall be there!"

"Right-o, Gwen. Um, where'd Jinkies go off to?" There was a pitiful mewling from above. Bianca looked up to find her kitty dangling from the parlor's unlit chandelier. "Jinkies! Get down from there this instant!"

"Mrrow?"

"Yes, right now!"

The witch would later claim that the cat's choice of landing spots was completely out of her control, but Selvi still didn't forgive her for a long time after. If anyone had asked the cat – which of course, no one had – they would have learned that the little feline liked the smell of the half-orc's hair. That's why he'd aimed directly for her braided scalp with all four sets of claws leading the way.

The woods behind the main keep of the Academy were surprisingly large for something found within castle walls. Gwenevrael had often wondered why Lady Amberyll even bothered. The mass of trees and brush would only help invaders if the castle were attacked. Then again, if the maps were right, then there was nobody around to attack the school, and as Bianca had discovered firsthand, there were magical defenses in place as well.

"Wishin' we could just go through the front gate," Selvi groused. "Prolly be safer."

"When was the last time you saw that way to be open?" the ranger replied. "Everything always comes through the Wayhouse doors. In any case, the heaviest defenses would need to be there as well. Watching spells, guardians, stuff like that. If we sneak over the wall back here, we're less likely to trip something."

"Mebbe, mebbe not," said the half-orc. "Don't forget what happened to the witchy-girl."

"Trust me; I haven't. She was flying high over the walls. We won't be." "So, what are we looking for?" asked Flora.

Gwenevrael thought about it. "A spot where the trees block the view of the wall from the keep and where there's a safe place to climb to on the other side."

Flora nodded, then cupped her hands. As she held them up near her face, Mr. Chitters hopped on. The druid let out a long string of clicks and squeaks, sometimes puffing up her cheeks to help get the sounds right.

"Um, she's talkin' to the squirrel again..." "Shush; let her do her thing."

Mr. Chitters was listening intently, with every sign of understanding more of the conversation than either princess. He gave a high-pitched "Chook!" and leapt from his mistress's hands, bounding off into the woods.

"Follow that squirrel!" shouted Flora. She took off after her pet, leaving the other two princesses to stare at her trail of dust.

"Look, it'll be easy," said Bianca. "Most of the teachers are off to one place or another, just like the other princesses. The rest are more like Mistress Heyerwif and never leave their part of the Academy 'cept for emergencies. We just need to do this fast."

The two girls were hiding around the corner from the entrance to the main teachers' lounge, which was tucked into one corner of the third floor. There was no sign that anyone was inside.

"Alright. Jinkies?" The little black cat perked at the sound of her voice. "Go reconnoiter."

"Mrow?"

Bianca sighed. "Go check it out." "Mrewl!"

"Pretty please? With anchovies on top?"

The cat considered for a moment, then padded away nonchalantly, as if it were by mere coincidence that he was going the way she had asked. He nosed around the door, sniffing and rubbing his chin against the hard wood. With a yawn, he sat down in a pool of sunlight that poured in from a nearby window, rolled over on his back, and stretched.

"Um... so, is it okay?" asked Cassandrella.

"It'd better be, or someone's not getting his treat tonight." Bianca tiptoed up to the door and tried the handle. "Locked," she said.

"Should we go get someone with a key?"

"You're not quite getting the idea here, Cassie. Only a teacher would have the key, but if it's locked, then at least no one's probably in there." Bianca sighed. "Didn't want to have to do this, but..."

The witch searched her pockets, coming up with a pin and a thin scrap of paper.

Her usual smile had turned upside down. "What are you..."

"Shhh. This is a spell that Gran'Mama taught me, so be quiet before I chicken out." She heard Cassie squeak in surprise right as she stabbed her thumb with the pin. A single drop of blood was squeezed out onto the paper. Bianca pressed the scrap to the door, where it stuck as if glued.

"By the pricking of my thumbs, something sneaky this way comes," the witch intoned. "Open locks, whoever knocks!" Lightly, she tapped on the door three times and heard the bolts turn inside it. With a click, it opened.

She motioned to Cassie, who was staring at her. "Well, shall we?" "W... w... that was witchcraft!"

"So it was. I'm a witch. What of it? Really? The broom and the hat should've been a tip-off."

"B-but, I thought that was all for show! To be cool or something. Ev-everyone knows witches are..."

"Can we continue this some other time when we're not standing in front of doors we shouldn't be going through?" Bianca grabbed the cleric and dragged her into the lounge.

The room was shabbier than she'd expected, full of threadbare old couches and stuffed chairs. There were cabinets for holding letters or papers and a flat mirror on one table that she recognized as having a facsimile charm on it.

"Hold on a moment." She crept over to where the files were stored. "What are you doing?" Cassie hissed at her.

Bianca ignored the cleric. Flipping through the alphabet of labels, she came across her name and pulled the file. She took a clean sheet of paper and placed it under the mirror, then pressed the main page of her file against the glass. She'd seen something like this before, and the memory rattled through her head like a many-sided die rolling a high number. There was a light buzz of magic at work, and the mirror flashed with a light that wasn't there. When she retrieved the paper from under it, the blank page was filled with Mistress Penskill's crabbed handwriting. Quickly, she copied the second page as well.

"Always wanted to know what the old bat thought of me," she said.

"Can we get out of here soon," pleaded Cassie. The poor thing's knees were trembling.

"Okay, okay, hold your bunnies." Bianca slipped over to the closet door. At this distance, she could feel the presence of her beloved broom within. She pulled at the latch, but it wouldn't open.

"Are you going to stick yourself again?"

"I can only do that trick once a day," she answered. "Watch the door, okay?"

The lock on this door wasn't nearly as good as the one on the main door.

Focusing her magic onto her singular lock of white hair, she made it grow and stretch, then directed it to slip around the edges of the door. It took a bit of fumbling, and she could feel her control slipping by the end, but she managed to jimmy the door open.

And there it was—her broom. A yard and a half of polished elm wood with a leather saddle running half its length, fitted to allow for two riders if they didn't mind being close. "Yes!" she cried softly, hugging it.

"Okay, time to go," she said to the cleric. "And I owe you a moonlit ride for coming with me here."

"Yeah..." Cassie didn't sound too happy about that anymore. Also: "Were you crying?"

"No!"

"Only, there's a tear on your cheek." "It's dusty in here, that's all..."

Jinkies blinked as his mistress and her silly friend shut the door and quietly slipped down the hall. Flicking his ears, which was to him what a shrug was to a human, he got up from his comfortable spot in the sun and followed them.

"Okay, so whaddawe got?" Selvi asked of the assembled princesses. Since they'd already gone through the trouble of making their bags already, it hadn't taken long to put together some basic travel packs. Only Cassandrella had really complained about leaving most of the clothing behind.

Five packs were gathered under the old oak tree, though one was technically hanging from a floating broomstick. Selvi's bag was sensibly done, as was the half- elf's, though she hated to give Princess Pointy-Ears any sort of compliment. The others... were serviceable, if hard to understand. Selvi'd never seen anything like some of the things sticking out of them.

"Got my broom, my cauldron, and my magic rod," announced Bianca. "I'm good to go!"

"What does the rod do?" asked Cassandrella.

"Darned if I know, but I'm going to figure it out eventually." "How 'bout you, Moonie?" asked Selvi.

"My travel robes, my moon-silver chain vest, and my moon scepter. For Love and Justice!" The girl twirled the scepter in the air.

"... Right. And you, Flora?"

The druid's pack was almost as pragmatic as hers, except for the lute and the staff planted in the ground next to it. That last one was the real oddity. Selvi could about swear that the thing was growing branches.

"My Staff of Plenty," said Flora. "Once it's set in the earth, it cannot be moved by anything or anyone except another druid. If given time, it will form branches and give us delicious fruit for breakfast."

"Handy," commented Gwenevrael. "And between myself and Selvi, we've got enough rope, canvas, and other materials to make camping a snap."

"I got a big picnic basket from the kitchen!" Cassandrella announced. "The cook felt sorry for us getting stuck here."

"Good. Let's get goin' then," said the barbarian. "Times a wastin'."

According to the druid's tree-rodent, the best spot to slip over the wall was along the southeast edge of the school grounds. Frankly, she wasn't so sure. There were some decent handholds, including a large dent in the stones about twenty feet up, but it wouldn't be an easy climb for at least two of them -- and that wasn't even counting the need to get the packs over.

"Well, girls. This is going to take a plan. Any ideas?"

After a fair amount of discussion, a fair bit more of arguing, and some fairly crude sketches in the dirt, they had one.

"What?" Uncle's face at this moment was a perfect picture. His eyebrows had levitated all the way up to the hairline, and his jaw had dropped just as far in the opposite direction. Under his right eye, the muscles along the cheekbone had bunched up and were twitching slightly. All of this had come from a single look at the plan, laid out carefully on a piece of scratch paper in colored pencil. The game had adjourned for a few minutes while he'd gone to the toilet and refilled his root beer, but then he'd returned to find... this. "Are you serious?"

"It's a good plan!" Helen insisted. "Definitely gonna work," said Cynthia.

"And didn't you tell us we should pool our resources?" added Shelby.

"Yes, but..." But he hadn't imagined anything like the Rube Goldberg scenario before him now. Okay, maybe it wasn't quite so bad as that, but it was close. "So... Bianca's going to fly up the wall, but not over it..."

"That's right!"

"And she's going to use her mud ball spell to fill a space in the rocks —" One that he'd intended to be used for a grapnel... " — and then stick Flora's Staff of Plenty in sideways?"

Katelyn nodded.

"You said that nothing could move it once it was planted," Shelby pointed out. "And it's magic, so 'nothing' could include gravity, right?"

"Before that," he continued, rubbing his head, "You'll wrap a section of canvas around the staff, rolled up at the edges, and once it's stuck in the wall, you'll hang a rope over it and use it as a pulley to lift all your gear up the wall?"

"Once Gwen and Flora have used it to climb up," said Helen.

"Cassie and Bianca are using the broom to get to the top but not go over," said Claire. "So we don't set off the gargoyles. Probably."

"Then I uses her awesome barbarian strength to hoist up the supplies so that everyone can unload them on top. She'll follow on up, and then we'll lower a rope down the other side to climb down," Shelby said. "Piece of cake."

"If you say so..." Honestly, he could think of a lot of ways this could go wrong, not to mention several things he could do as the game master to prevent them from succeeding. Things he probably should do, like point out that the mud ball spell shouldn't produce enough mud to make this work, just to keep things within the letter of the rules. But... it was the most creative thing he'd seen from them so far, and it wasn't even the craziest thing he'd ever seen in a game. Plus, he could smell the pizzas cooking in Max's oven.

His stomach made the decision for him. "Okay, I'll allow it: time to roll 'em, ladies. Katelyn, Bianca's skill bonus for flying will be canceled out by having to balance Cassie on there as well, so you will need to secure her somehow. Cynthia, Flora doesn't have any points in climbing, so use her strength bonus when you roll. There's no rush on most of this, so if at first you don't succeed, I'll let you take ten. That is," he explained, "we'll imagine it takes longer than normal, but you do finally reach the top.

Okay, let's roll."

The view from the wall was rather nice, Gwenevrael thought. The forest extended a long way into the distance, where it met the hazy purple outline of the eastern mountains. Her eyes picked out more landmarks, matching them to the map in her hands. There was the lake and the river... She relaxed. Everything seemed accurate so far.

Behind her, she could hear Selvi grunting as she pulled Flora up the last few feet. The druid had gone back down to retrieve her staff but then needed help getting back up while holding on to the cumbersome thing.

"So, we ready to go?" asked Bianca. The witch had somehow managed to ferry Cassandrella without dropping her, though the cleric had not liked the idea of being strapped in by magically animated hair. The moon princess's face was green like cheese as Bianca's white lock released her, and she fell off the broom and onto the stone of the walls.

"Just a moment..." Cassandrella burped. "Not feeling so good..."

The ranger secured the rope onto a stone fixture, after first making sure it wasn't a gargoyle or otherwise some potential defense of the school, and tossed it off the other side. The rope didn't quite reach the bottom, but it came within a few feet. Nearby, Flora's squirrel chittered at her.

"Okay; you were right, sir squirrel. I am sorry to have doubted you," she said in a low voice. The last thing she needed was for Selvi to see her talking with the little red rodent.

Getting back down the wall on the other side wasn't nearly as difficult, though once again, they had to secure Cassandrella properly before lowering her down in the same manner as the packs. The moon princess was not happy by the time they got her to the ground, but at least they were all outside the walls now.

She nodded to Selvi, and the half-orc nodded back. The two of them hefted their packs and helped the magic-users with theirs. Then, as a group, they began their adventure.

"And it's time for a pizza break!" Uncle announced. "Katelyn, that was some very good role-playing with Bianca and Claire? You added some excellent details. We're going to have to capitalize on those in the future."

"My princess didn't get to do much," said Cynthia with a pout.

"We'll just have to fix that after we have our pizza, eh?" Uncle winked. "Don't worry; you're headed into a forest. Druids always have things to do in the forest. And," he added before Shelby could form the words. "There will be fights. It's time for some action."

"Good." The black-haired girl nodded at that. "Enjoying it so far?"

"Yeah, Uncle!" "Uh-huh!" "... yes." "Super-fantastic!" "It's okay." "Thanks for the ringing endorsement, ladies."

Max had the pies set on the neighboring table, and the ravenous horde of princess players migrated in that direction with nary a complaint. Uncle tidied the game table, swapping out a generic forest map for the one of the castle, and made some notes from the safety of his game-master's screen. The sturdy cardboard divider was what hid most of the game's important information from the players, and in his head, Uncle imagined a scene that must have played out behind closed doors, where no princesses were allowed.

"And there they go." Mistress Penskill tapped the edge of her magic mirror, making the image within both larger and clearer. The Academy's main instructor in the arts arcane was short and round, with bright aqua hair and a serious, sour face that did not jive with her gnomish heritage at all. She shook her head as she watched the five young students disappear into the forest. "Is this such a good idea to let them off the leash like this?"

"It will be pleasingly quiet here, ja?" said Mistress Heyerwif. "Those girls would find some trouble und make us all go crazy."

"They will need to learn how to work together, to trust one another," said Lady Amberyll. The headmistress leaned back in her chair and massaged her temples. "That is not something we can teach at this institution. If we were to try, we would most likely achieve the opposite result. No, no," she said. "Let it be their own choices which instruct them. We shall enjoy the show and intervene only if absolutely necessary."

Mistress Penskill nodded, and the image in the mirror faded away. "Still can't believe that little pipsqueak had the temerity to steal copies from our files."

"I did warn you." Lady Amberyll's eyes glittered with amusement. "That is why we only put what we wanted her to see in that file, was it not?"

"Sure, sure. Hope you know what game you're playing here. That one's grandmother is no joke."

"Neither am I, Penelope. Neither am I."

Pizza Time!

Chapter 3

The Quest Begins

Okay!" Uncle called. "Are we ready to keep going?"

A low rumble of general assent floated to his ears from the far side of the table, fueled by pizza grease and sugary drinks. Everyone had certainly had their fill of Max's signature pepperoni-plus pizza. He would have to step things up before they went into a food coma.

"So, to recap: Five young princesses, played by you ladies, have just snuck out of school because you all didn't want to be stuck there for the entire summer. As far as the game is concerned, that all happened yesterday now. You managed to make decent time that first day, then Gwen and Selvi set up camp for the night. The next day, you get up fairly early and keep going. So now you're in the middle of a big wild forest. What are you going to do?"

He expected Cynthia to chime in first, or Helen. Their princesses certainly had the most skills related to traveling through the woods. Shelby was also a possibility since the girl had been taking charge a lot so far. But no, once again, his expectations were dashed upon the reality that these kids were nothing like him and certainly were not playing the game the same way.

"We stop at noon to have a picnic!" Claire shouted before anyone else could say anything.

"A... picnic."

"Yeah! We got a picnic basket from the school kitchen, and it was so full of stuff that we couldn't eat it all yesterday, so today we should have a picnic!"

"Wouldn't we eat it all for breakfast?" said Shelby. "That's a very good po--"

"But Flora's got that magic staff!" Cynthia interrupted him. "We'd have lots of fresh fruit for breakfast so that we could save the leftovers for lunch."

Everyone was nodding at this, much to Uncle's annoyance. He looked over the notes behind his divider screen, where the details for a fight with some bandits lay. As encounters went, it was pretty straightforward, especially for level three characters, but he'd wanted to ease the girls into this. Now, though? If they wanted picnics, he'd give them...

Hmm... Uncle keyed in a quick internet search, coming up with all the details he needed before the girls could even finish debating how to do the picnic. "Alright, ladies," he announced. "It's picnic time, with everything that goes along with it."

It was a beautiful day in the forest. The sun shone down on them through the trees, and the birds were singing like a choir of angels. For a temple-raised girl like Princess Cassandrella, it was like a fairy tale turned real. She hopped and skipped merrily down the trail, stopping every few minutes to ask Gwenevrael or Flora for the name of some flower that had caught her eye.

The ranger and the druid put up with her exuberance, though Selvi rolled her eyes every time. The barbarian didn't have much use for flowers.

Bianca was the least happy of the lot because it turned out that she did have to walk after all. The twisty forest trails were hard to navigate by broom, and she was always dragging her feet in the dirt or hitting her head on branches. The broom followed her around instead, carrying her pack and Jinkies, who was happily perched on the saddle, how she envied the little fuzzbutt.

"Can we stop and rest for a bit?" she whined. "My feet are killing me!" "Yeah!" chimed in Cassie. "And it's almost time for lunch, too!"

"We took a break an hour ago," growled Selvi. "Can't you --" She was stopped by Gwenevrael's hand on her shoulder.

"A group travels only as fast as its slowest member," the ranger pointed out. "And it is a good time of day to have a meal."

"Picnic time!" crowed the moon princess.

"Yeah, yeah." Selvi brushed the hand away. "Coddle the softies, why dontcha.

Their poor widdle toes might fall off their feet, otherwise."

"Really?" Cassandrella sat on the nearest rock, pulled off a boot, and wiggled her toes. "Nope, all present and accounted for!"

"It looks like there might be a clearing ahead," Flora announced, ignoring the discussion entirely. "What's left in the basket?"

There was quite a lot left in the big wicker basket they'd received from the Academy cook. Either Mistress Fresnelding had been extra generous, or she'd overestimated how much the five girls could eat. Flora's Staff of Plenty had produced handfuls of fuzzy brown fruits, all green and juicy on the inside, to break their morning fast, so the bread, cheese, and sausage inside the basket could wait till now.

The glen was perhaps twenty feet across, and its ground was covered with soft green grass. A few rocks poked through the turf and served as excellent shelves for heavy packs. Selvi unfurled a roll of tent canvas upon the ground, and the five of them settled down for an enjoyable lunch. There were enough sandwich fixings for everyone, with a bit of sausage left over for Jinkies.

Flora had her lute out and was happily assaulting everyone's ears with off-key caroling when she wasn't cramming ham and cheese in her face. Jinkies yowled along a few times.

Yes, a good time was had by all, right up to when cat and squirrel sat up stock straight, with ears pricked and noses twitching.

"Um, Helen? Why's your uncle chuckling like that?" asked Shelby. "I dunno. Er, Uncle? Uncle..."

It was a huge smile, a massive grin plastered across his face. His friends had often told him never to play poker, which was fine by him. This was more his game, and it was time to pull the ace from his sleeve. "Well, ladies. You wanted a picnic, and where there's a picnic, there's also... them."

"Them?" Cynthia gave him the screwy eye, which only made him grin harder. "Yup. Them."

Chapter 4

THEM

The princesses were looking every which way, trying to figure out where the trouble was coming from. Something was obviously setting the animals on edge, but what? Selvi and Cassandrella hopped to their feet and looked down the trail while Gwenevrael's eyes scanned the high tree branches. Flora and Bianca were trying to calm their critters with little success. Mr. Chitters and Jinkies were shaking from nerves.

And when trouble came, it wasn't from the trail, nor the trees. With a great push, something forced its way up from under the picnic canvas, sending the two remaining princesses and their pets tumbling away. The canvas jumped and shook, flapping away to reveal... them.

Three bodies, each the size of a large dog, covered in reddish-brown fuzz. Broad, rounded heads with large, glittery eyes, short antenna, and clicking mandibles. Six skinny, hard-shelled legs, the first two of which sported four-clawed hands with opposable thumbs.

More followed from the hole they'd opened beneath the canvas.

"Ants?!"

"What's a picnic without them?" Uncle laughed. "And now I feel like watching old monster movies. Well, ladies? They caught you off guard. Whatcha gonna do?"

Gwenevrael wasn't sure what to make of... Them. They were ants, but on the other hand, not. Regular ants weren't three and a half feet long. They also didn't immediately grab people's packs and... wait, what?

"What!?" she shouted. "Stop! Stop them! Selvi! Cassandrella!"

There were ten of them out of the hole now, and they'd paired off to grab the princesses' gear. Faster than anyone could react, the ant-things were hustling their loot away.

"Hey!" Selvi recovered from surprise the fastest, jumping in to block the pair of ants with her pack. In her head, she was cussing long and hard that she'd left her sword next to her stuff. The scimitar was in the hands of Them, now.

"Shelby, language."

The black-haired girl just blew him a raspberry.

Selvi Khan's-daughter was a champion of êl-sakhar, a sport of the high plains played traditionally with the severed heads of one's enemies, though nowadays it was usually a weighted ball of rags instead. Either way, these ant things weren't nearly as heavy, and with a single swift kick, she punted the one with her sword into the nearest tree. As she reclaimed the blade, she could see Princess Point-Ears wresting her bow and quiver from another pair of marauders. Moonie wasn't having as much luck freeing her pack, though it was fun watching her whack a bug over the head repeatedly with her holy symbol and yelling things like "Moon's Justice!"

The witch girl shouted a bunch of words, through their meaning was lost on Selvi's ears. The magic broom understood, apparently, and it leaped from the grasp of an ant-thing. Bianca's pack tried to follow along, pulled by the straps, but a quick snip of the mandibles cut it off. The broom flew freely back to its mistress with the little cauldron dangling from it. The rest of the pack disappeared down the trail with the ants.

"After them!" Selvi roared, baring her tusks in anger. How dare these... these bugs steal from them! She would squish their heads beneath her boots, rip their legs from their thoraxes and beat war drum rhythms on their fat, buggy butts! Her rage pushed her forward down the path, paying no attention to the whipping branches or protruding roots, or --

Something slammed into her from behind, forcing her to the ground. She almost sent a fist smashing right into the other person's face before she realized it was Princess Pointy-Ears.

Oh, who was she kidding? Selvi wanted to punch the half-elf anyway.

"What are you..." she began, but Gwenevrael shushed her and pointed up. A rather large and heavy-looking log came swinging across the trail and through the space where Selvi would have been. A second later, it swung back, not quite as fast.

"Those buggies are smarter than they look," the ranger said. "Had their escape planned out really well."

"Er, yeah." As her anger and rage receded, Selvi realized just how dumb she'd been. This did not make her any happier. "Thanks," she said through gritted teeth.

"Don't get me wrong," said Gwenevrael. "I still don't like you, and I know you still don't like me, but if we're going to get our stuff back, then we shall need to work together." The half-elf offered a gloved hand. "A continued truce?"

Selvi took the hand and shook it. "Yeah, for now."

"So, what did we lose?" Gwenevrael asked once everyone was back in the clearing.

"All of our packs," Flora reported, "and the picnic basket, too. They tried to take my Staff of Plenty but couldn't get it out of the ground. Left the canvas," she added as an afterthought.

"At least we got our weapons," growled Selvi. Gwenevrael could only nod at that.

"Got my broom, too!" Bianca announced. "But... but..." The little witch's eyes began to tear up. "My magic rod was in my pack! Gran'Mama gave it to me and told me to keep it safe and be a smart girl and figure it out, and now she's going to be so mad, and what am I going to do? WAAAAAAAHH!" She broke down as the other princesses stared.

Cassandrella plopped down to the witch's left and Flora to her right, then the two of them squished her in the middle of the biggest hug they could manage. The sniffly sobs were smothered in folds of homespun cotton and shimmery moon-silk.

"Okay, okay. Mushy stuff aside," said Selvi. "What are we doin' to get our stuff back?" The barbarian growled. "Shoulda kept chasin' them."

"And you'd soon have discovered just how many traps they've set on that trail." "Yeah, yeah. Rub it in, why dontcha."

"If you would permit this intrusion, ladies..." A voice, long and sinuous on the vowels and slightly lisped on the esses, slipped through the mass of trees behind the princesses to surprise them as a light tickle on the ears.

Selvi had her scimitar up and ready, and Gwenevrael had an arrow nocked before the last ess could finish.

Something was standing in the shadows of the trees, though not even the half-elf's keen eyes could pick out the details at first. Some magic had kept it hidden from their sight, and that same magic made this person blurry and shadowed even as it walked towards them. Once the figure reached the sunlight of the clearing, the magic was dispelled, and the five princesses got a good look at their visitor.

The... person stood tall like a man, almost as tall as Princess Selvi, but was like nothing they'd ever seen before. The body was stocky, with short legs and long arms, and its fingers and toes were tipped with thick claws. Its face was snout-like, with long lips and a tiny nose. A scaly plate of natural armor spread from its forehead, over its crown, and down its back. Tufts of fur stuck out between the scales. A broad tail hung behind it, also scaled. This newcomer looked nothing so much like a pangolin crossed with a human.

"A what-o-lin?" asked Shelby.

"Yeah, what's that?" chimed in Claire. Behind her huge glasses, the girl's eyes twinkled curiously.

"Sounds familiar..." said Cynthia.

"Y'know, a pangolin," said Uncle. "They've got some down at the zoo. Kind of like an armadillo, but with scales instead of banded armor. They can roll up into balls," he added.

"Aw yeah, that's the one!"

-tickety tappety tap- Uncle had his laptop out. "Look, this is what I'm talking about," he said, pulling up a Wikipedia page for the animals. That was followed by an internet video of baby pangolins for the girls to coo over while he grabbed some more root beer.

"Okay, ladies," he said when he returned. "Whatcha gonna do?" "Attack it!" said Shelby.

"No!" said Helen. "He hasn't done anything yet." "He was pretty polite..." added Claire.

"... let's ask."

"Okay!" said Shelby. "My princess doesn't lower her sim, shim..." "Scimitar."

"Right. Doesn't lower her simmy-tar, but she asks him what he's doing. Um, it is a 'him,' right?"

Uncle shrugged. "Hard to say, just by looking. The voice sounds more masculine, though. Anyhoo, the pangolin-man greets you again and introduces himself as L'shoopfloopshup."

"Wow, say that again!" Claire said. "L'shoopfloopshup."

"Ten times fast!" demanded Helen.

"L'shoopfloopshuplshoopshupfloopshup.
.." Uncle screwed his face up, crossed his eyes,
and stuck out his tongue, much to the
amusement of the girls. "But you can call him
Louis," he said. "Please."

"Okay, um, Louis," said Gwenevrael as
she relaxed the hold on her bowstring.

The magically produced arrow shaft
flickered and disappeared, no longer
necessary. "It is good to hear a friendly voice,
but I must ask. What are you doing here?"

"If I may?" The pangolin man sat on the
dirt with his tail curled up around his legs. "I
am traveling with a band of my brothers and
sisters. We wander the world, hunting down
tasty insects for food and sport. Perhaps you
can guess where this is heading?"

"Them," Flora said with a scowl. "The
ants. They ain't natural, are they?

Something felt wrong."

"Ah yes, you are a daughter of the
woods, are you not? No, the ant-men are not a

result of nature's path, though if I am to be honest, neither are my people."

"The forest ain't afraid of you, though." Beside the druid, Mr. Chitters gave his squeak of approval.

"And happy am I to hear that. The truth is, my comrades and I have been tracking this contingent of the ant-men for some time now. They appear to have settled in these woods, and we believe they are preparing to contact their queen at the home hive. Should that happen, then an invasion may be imminent. It occurs to me that, as natives of this land and recent victims of their rapacious nature, you might desire some aid and give the same in return?"

"What the heck's that supposed to mean?" asked Selvi.

"He's saying that we can all help each other," said the ranger.

"Why doesn't he just do it himself?" The half-orc eyed the pangolin man suspiciously.

"It is enough to say that the numbers do not favor my band," said Louis. "The workers are of little concern, were there not so many of them. Then there are the warriors, which are a much more difficult matter. And the leader of the outpost, well... Even with the assistance of you ladies, we will have our hands busy."

"But we'll get our stuff back?" asked Bianca. The tears had dried, but her eyes were still red and angry.

"That, and whatever else you may want from their hoard," promised Louis. "My people's objective is death to the ants. We care not for the rest."

Gwenevrael nodded. "I think we can agree to these terms." Beside her, Selvi wasn't looking happy, but the barbarian wasn't saying no, either.

"Good." Louis hopped to his feet and bowed. "If you would follow me to my camp, where we can rest and prepare?"

The princesses grabbed everything that was left to them and followed the pangolin man into the forest.

"So when you get to his camp," Uncle was saying, "you see six more of Louis's friends doing various things. They don't all look like him; some are more armadillo-ish, while others look like anteaters or even hedgehogs.

They introduce themselves, but all the names are just as hard to pronounce."

"What are we doing now?" asked Cynthia. "Preparing, I guess," Claire answered. "But how?"

Shelby raised her hand. "I'm gonna talk with someone to make battle plans."

"Magic users should also take time to make sure their spells are ready," Uncle noted. "Er, yes?" Katelyn was tugging on his sleeve. "What is it?" The girl pointed to a note on her sheet. "Okay, Bianca can make some potions, too. One of Louis's friends will help there."

"I'll ask Mr. Chitters to help me find some animals to help us!" offered Cynthia. "Gwen will go with Selvi to talk with Louis and his boss," said Helen.

Uncle clapped his hands. "Well then, sounds like we've got stuff to do!"

Chapter 5

The Battle

"Fifty buggers, you say?" Selvi was staring at a rough map of the area, drawn in reddish-brown ink on animal skin. It was simply done, with little triangles for trees and circles for rocks, but it still looked more accurate than the one the princesses had.

"Plus five warriors, the leader, and three others besides." Louis's leader was a long-nosed, shaggy person with light cream and brown fur. His voice was booming and nasal, and his name had been officially shortened to Phil.

"What others?" Gwenevrael leaned in, tracing the map with one of her knives. "The leader caste of the ant-men like to keep pets," explained Louis. "A few days

back, the ants caught a few bandits. The fools were trying to steal food, I imagine. In

any case, they're working for the bugs now, whether they like it or not."

"Which is why your assistance is appreciated," said Phil. "The three pets are strong in ways we cannot work well against. But they do not see well in the dark, which is why we shall wait till late in the evening to attack."

The ranger nodded. "I can see in the darkness, and I believe half-orcs can as well, right?"

Selvi grunted.

"That still leaves the others, though..."

Claire had her hand raised and waving frantically. The tips of her oversized hair ribbon wobbled like a pair of floppy ears.

"Yes, Claire?" Uncle didn't quite sigh.

"Since my magic is all holy moon power and stuff, do I have a spell that lets people see in the dark?"

"No, that's not a cleric's spell usually..."

"Can I ask for it anyway?" She pulled nervously on her glasses. "Ask me?"

"No, ask the Moon." The little girl stood on her seat so they could look eye to eye. "Can I ask the Moon for a spell like that?"

Uncle considered for a moment, then made a quick calculation on a piece of scrap paper. "Okay. Since your goddess is actually in the sky right now, visible and about half full, I guess you can ask her for a boon. Roll your big one, add in your wisdom modifier -- that's a plus three, by the way -- and we shall see."

A goldenrod orange twenty-sided die clattered across the table, coming up 19. "Whew..." Uncle whistled. "And with the modifier, that's a twenty-two. Okay

then, you get a new trick in your level two spell slot, instead of one use of Align

Weapon. It's called, um..." "Moon Eyes Shine Bright!"

"Er, sure. Let's go with that. It grants low-light vision to yourself and two other people, for one night."

"Thanks, Uncle game-dude!"

Flora sat on a tree stump at the edge of the camp, listening to the sound of the woods. Birdsong had faded with the light of day, to be replaced with the buzz of insects. It was easy to meditate and open her mind to the voice of nature -- and wow, was it an angry one. She could hear it in the bristling of the pine needles, in shrieks of the hawk, and the whining of mosquitoes. There was something in these woods that the woods did not want, and this princess knew what that thing was. She cradled her lute and strummed along to the magic in her head, calling out to all the little ears that were willing to hear.

She'd been correct earlier. Nature absolutely hated those ant-men, as much as it could hate anything. With a pluck and a twang of the lute string, she told Nature exactly what was upsetting it and how to make it stop.

Bianca spent most of the afternoon with a hard-shelled member of the anti-bug squad named Mmshuthrashl. The witch called her Mim. Mim was the healer of the group, and had dozens of little bags of spell components on hand. Bianca's little cauldron was put to good use, and soon she was filling a dozen tiny vials with a light green liquid.

"This one's full of jumping magic," she was explaining to a wide-eyed Cassie. "Slurp one down, and you'll be bouncing like a bunny rabbit for a few minutes." She waved to the other colors they'd already finished. "Blue is Mim's special health potion. Everyone's getting two of those."

Cassie took her share of the green and blue, tucking them into the pockets of her moon-silk robe. "What about this?" she asked, reaching for a vial of red liquid.

A pale, slender hand grabbed the cleric's wrist. The little witch was stronger than she looked, and her face was deadly serious. "Mim made that one for me, special. That one's dangerous, and it's all mine," was all she said.

The moon princess looked into her friend's eyes and saw all the tales of witches reflected within them. She couldn't help but shiver a little.

Now it was late into the night. The Moon had come and almost left, sinking slowly behind the mountains. Some of its glow remained in the night sky, along with thousands of twinkling stars. Bianca knew the constellations well, and thanks to Cassie's new spell, she could see well enough by their light to navigate above the tree-tops with ease.

To the north, beneath the constellation of the Dragon with its burning red eye, there was a clearing. Flora had described it quite well. All of the trees there had recently been chopped down and chewed up by the ant-men, and now a gaping hole opened in the middle.

She was flying over the hole right now. It was a deep black circle in the middle of the dirt and grass. Bianca carefully pulled out one of the red potions, held it out at arm's length, and let it fall.

With a whoomph, the hole was no longer dark and black. She liked it better in bright red though she barely dodged the rising fireball.

There was the signal! The fading moonlight was as bright as day thanks to Cassandrella's magic, and to Princess Flora's eyes the explosion was brighter still. She could see ants from where she was perched, high in a tree. Louis said the buggers couldn't see too well by night, and she trusted him on that. She trusted her new furry friends more.

Flora raked her fingers across her lute with a loud twang. As loudly as she could, she sang:

>My eyes have seen the horror
>>of the coming of the squirrels!
>With their sharp-sharp teeth
>>and bushy tails, they aid us pretty girls.
>With the rabbits and the deer,
>>they make those buggies hurl!
>Fuzzy-wuzzies rule the world!

Not half bad for an afternoon's composition if she did say so herself. From the bushes all around the clearing, the fuzzy-wuzzies burst into action, descending on the worker ants as they poured from the fiery depths of their hill. Anyone who thought rabbits were weak had never seen a mother bunny take on a snake in defense of her young. Those teeth weren't just there for nibbling carrots!

"Um, thank you for the musical selection, Cynthia," said Uncle. "With your encouragement, all the local squirrels and rabbits are busy biting legs off of workers while the deer are trampling the bodies." He rolled a die behind his divider screen. "Your 'Battle Hymn of the Fuzzy-Wuzzies' even attracted a badger, which is currently trashing a squad of worker ants by the north end of the clearing." A red piece of plastic marked the spot. "Let's just give him some space, 'kay? Badgers aren't the friendliest sorts."

"Wow, that was awesome!" shouted Cynthia. "Thanks for lettin' me try it."

"No prob, kiddo." Honestly, he'd stretched the definitions of most of the animal-handling spells and skills on that one, but she'd rolled well, and it really was funnier this way. "So, who's up next?"

Arrows flashed overhead, streaking through the air from where Princess Pointy-Ears was hiding. Selvi scowled. Just like an elf to stay in the trees where it was safe.

She preferred to get down and dirty. Brandishing her scimitar, Selvi Khan's-daughter screamed defiantly and rushed into the chaos.

Ahead of her, an armadillo man was barreling through the worker ants, leaving wide gaps in the enemy's defenses for her to pass. Behind her, Moonie and the rest of the bug-eaters followed. Her ears told her that, though she kept her eyes forward.

The little bugs were no challenge at all and dangerous only because they wouldn't stop for anything. Her scimitar cut them down left and right, while her boots stomped bug bits with loud crunches.

One. Stomp. Two. Stomp. Three. Stomp... This was maybe the most boring fight of her young life!

With a shriek, more ants swarmed from the hill. These newcomers were twice the size of the workers and looked even bigger when they stood tall and upright on four legs. Thick forearms wielded nasty-looking spears, shields, or axes.

"Awright!" the barbarian shouted. "Now that's more like it!"

Unlike the half-orc, Princess Cassandrella hadn't been in a real fight even once in her entire life. She had her moon-silver armor, yes, and her scepter doubled wonderfully as a head-thumper, but that didn't mean she was in any way prepared.

Mistress Mehl's basic combat course at the Academy hadn't included anything about giant bugs, for crying out loud! Someone should make a complaint, she decided.

But first, there was the problem at hand. When the warrior ants made their appearance, all clicking jaws and waving spears, of course, she was scared! Who wouldn't be? And when she was scared, there was only one thing for a young moon princess to do. She prayed.

"O Bounteous Moon! Grant me thy light so that I may squish some buggy butt!"

Her blessed mother may not have approved of that prayer, but the Moon didn't seem to mind. Cassandrella's scepter glowed with a soft silver light, and then it was gone, replaced by a piece of the shining moon in the shape of a sword.

"Moonlight Crescent Cut!"

Princess Fiona finished her song with a flourish to signal that it was time for all fuzzy animals to make themselves scarce. Most of them listened if they hadn't already scampered away, but that old badger on the north side continued fighting and biting like a hungry man battling for the last plate of flapjacks.

"Stay here, Mr. Chitters," she commanded. "No, you're not coming along," she added when the squirrel chittered back. "You'd just be... What do you mean, I'd be in the way too!?"

She dropped to the ground and hefted her lute. The ants may have made off with her pack and the simple sword within it, but she still had this. It was made of enchanted ironwood and strong enough to take a hit or give one. Her favorite uncle had given it to her, along with some magic words. She'd never tried them, but now it seemed like as good a time as any...

"El Kabong!"

The wood of the lute swelled and stretched until it was a huge, spiked club. It still weighed the same in her hands, but she bet it would hurt ants just the same.

"El Kabong?" Shelby had one eyebrow raised in perfect derision. "Seriously?" "That's the problem with kids these days," groused Uncle. "No appreciation for the classics."

"If you can call it that." The curly-haired girl rolled her eyes. "And what's with all the magic stuff, all of a sudden?"

"Well, I gave you all this cool stuff at the beginning, and not all of it has seen use.

Speaking of which, aren't you the least bit curious what your special item does?"

All five of the warriors were out and about now, and everyone had their hands full. Louis and Phil had taken the first, slashing at it with their claws, while the rolling armadillo and a spiky echidna-man fended off another.

Selvi's attention was on the reddish-brown monstrosity before her. This warrior bore a sword and shield, both fashioned from some sort of shell. Whatever the stuff was, her blade couldn't get a bite into it. Each hit slid off with a soft clang. She hacked and slashed, only to be parried and blocked at each turn.

It was playing with her! Selvi's moonlit vision began to turn red in fury. How dare it treat her like... like... a child! A weakling! Could it not tell she was a khan's daughter, a warrior by blood!? Rage burned within her, kindling a flame in her chest, centered on the dragonbone talisman around her neck.

The polished knucklebone was carved with the names of her ancestors, great warriors all, and though she couldn't look down to check, she was certain that those names now glowed like dragon's fire. The spirits of her forefathers fought with her, she knew, and Selvi pressed on even harder.

And then, to her left and to her right, glowing red forms appeared, bearing arms and armor much like hers. On the left was an orcish warrior, glorious and strong, while on the right was a human of the high plains, with a spiked turban and oiled beard. Both wielded the wickedly curved blades of her homeland, and as one, they moved with her.

Try as it might, the warrior ant could not stop three blades at once. With a wild howl, the barbarian princess pressed the advantage.

"And that's how the ancestral totem power works for you," Uncle was explaining. "The spirits move with you, attack with you, basically give you three sword strokes for the price of one. However, they can't attack things independently, can't leave your side, and they only appear if you're raging while wearing that talisman."

"Okay, whatever." Shelby was trying to keep a cool look on her face and was failing. "I'm gonna keep attacking on my next turn."

"Alright. But first, could you roll your big one for me?" Uncle asked. "Everyone else, too?"

Shelby gave him her best puzzled-but-who-cares-what-you-think look but rolled anyway. The red twenty-sider rattled across the table, coming up 8. Everyone else rolled much higher, except for Claire's piddling 2.

"This was a perception check. It's meant to see if you're paying attention to other stuff in battle. The leader and her pets have just arrived." He placed a chess king, two knights, and a bishop on the table, not far from Selvi's pawn. "Unfortunately, a certain barbarian princess is too busy hacking things up to notice."

Selvi Khan's-daughter felt on top of the world. With furious howls she was slowly wearing down the warrior ant, and she anticipated with glee the final strike that would send its buggy carcass to the ground in pieces.

Then the wind picked up. It blew in hard from her right, raising trails of dust and leaves. A second later, she was off her feet, blown head over heels by a blast of rushing air. Her rage was broken by the distraction, and the two phantom fighters disappeared with it.

Up above, Princess Bianca saw everything. She saw where a new hole opened in the earth, and she saw the three human forms climb out to herald the arrival of the ant leader. She saw one of the former bandits raise a rod -- her rod! -- and blast Selvi with a huge gust of wind.

Most importantly, she saw how he did it.

Her magic lock of white hair grew long, draping down to the ground. With great care, she eased her broom forward, letting the hair float quietly along until it was brushing against the rod in the bandit's hand. Then, like a snake, she struck. Her hair plucked the magic heirloom from the man's surprised grasp.

The leader ant noticed her, raising its buggy head in all its horribly buggy glory.

Compared to the warriors, it was slender, almost dainty, with a tapered body and smaller mandibles. Its antennae were long and swept-back, and a series of horny bumps circled the flat space of its head like a tiara. With her improved vision, she could see the strangely human hands on the end of those ant arms make arcane gestures.

Sparks of light began to circle its wrists.

Oh, no. Bianca wasn't about to let a buggy wizard get the drop on her. She aimed her rod at it, tracing her fingers across the golden inlay the way she'd seen the bandit mage do, and --

Her world seemed to shatter as strange patterns filled her brain. Everything was precise and geometric, formed of pure shapes linked by the lightning of consciousness. It was too alien, too much, too loud inside her skull.

Bianca dropped from her broom like a stone.

Gwenevrael had stopped shooting arrows when Louis and their allies had moved in. Even with her elven eyesight, she couldn't be sure about her targets in all this chaos. It was all good, though; she still had her sword.

As did Cassandrella, the ranger was surprised to see. The moon princess was holding her own against a swarm of workers, waving around a blade of silvery light as if she actually knew how to use it. The weapon did not seem to cut the ants, but by their reactions, it was apparent something was hurting them.

Then a taller shadow loomed over the cleric. One of the warrior ants had come to the aid of its lesser brethren, and Cassandrella did not seem to notice the monster's axe as it was raised high above her head.

Gwenevrael would have cursed if she'd had the time to spare. Instead, she quickly drank one of Bianca's potions, a green one that almost made her gag. The stuff tasted like pure, concentrated awful, but it worked. She could feel the power in her legs as she leaped and bounded across the field, hurdling over worker ants and occasionally using them as springboards. The ranger landed next to the cleric just in time to deflect the warrior's axe with her own sword.

"I've got your back," she told the surprised princess. "Let's waste this one together."

Cassandrella nodded, and together they rushed the warrior. She jumped high, bringing her sword down on the ant's shield with a clash, while the moon princess took the opening and stabbed it in the thorax with her weapon. "Lovely Lunar Fixation!" the cleric cried as the oversized ant screamed in pain.

Gwenevrael was caught in the chest by a flailing arm -- the one with the shield, thankfully. The blow knocked the wind out of her, but she still managed to duck and roll, coming back on her feet almost immediately. The ant was hacking at Cassandrella, but the cleric was hopping like a crazed bunny rabbit, just barely dodging the first blow, then the second, only to get hit in the face by the shield.

With the last lingering effect of the potion's jumpiness lingering in her legs, Gwenevrael drew her daggers and leapt for the warrior's back. The bug wore a metal collar to protect its thin neck, but that wasn't much good for it now. The ranger brought her two daggers across the collar, and the neck snapped.

The rest of the ant collapsed to the ground with a thud.

"Are you alright?" Flora asked as she pulled Selvi up. Her lute had returned to its original form for now, though it proved more than good enough to bat a worker ant away all by itself.

Selvi wasn't sure how to answer. The heat of her rage had faded away, and now she felt cold inside. If the druid weren't right there to see it, she could have puked her guts out. "Er, yeah. Just fine and dandy," she lied. "Where's everyone else?"

"Cassie and Gwen are holding off one of the warrior ants that way." Flora pointed to the south. "Louis's people took out most of the rest, so now they're working on the leader."

"Wha.. Where's the one I was fighting?" If someone else had stolen her glory,

oh...

"It retreated to the other side of the hill, I think. Somewhere that way, at least. Looked like it was hurting plenty from the way you mauled it."

"Hmph." There was some satisfaction in that, at least. "What about witchy-girl?"

The druid shrugged. "Not sure. Saw her fall off her broom a little while back.

Found you first, though."

"Might as well find her, then." Selvi winced as her armor moved across several new bruises. "Gotta stick together'n all that."

Bianca was having the worst headache of her life. What had happened? Had the ant leader got her with some sort of magic attack? All she knew was that she would do anything for some of Gran'Mama's special headache cure right now, even though she knew exactly what the old bat put in it.

Up above, she could hear Jinkies mewling from the back of the broom. Without her, the flying stick was circling in a holding pattern, awaiting her command. It could wait a little longer she decided, at least until she could stand up straight without seeing double.

Four people were running up to her. No, wait. Two people. Selvi and Flora. Weakly, she waved.

"Hey, ladies. Got my magic rod back." Her voice sounded addled, even to her own ears. "Gran'Mama will be so happy with me."

"Good going... oh, crap!" shouted Selvi. The barbarian raised her scimitar.

Down the slope a ways, three figures could be seen stumbling through the evening dark. The leader ant's pets were having a difficult time of it, as the grass was now covered in bits of ant, and their eyes weren't as keen or as enchanted as the princesses'. They should have been cussing away every time they stepped in a puddle of buggy guts, but instead, the three bandits were strangely quiet.

"I got 'em," Bianca declared, aiming her rod at the first bandit. It only shook a little in her hands as she brought its magic to life. "Take this!" she shouted.

The bandit stopped dead in his tracks and screamed. Dropping his sword, he doubled over and clutched at the ground as his silhouette expanded and grew in the dim light of the evening. When he stood again, he was over twelve feet tall, and all of his gear had similarly grown with him.

"Um, so your grandmother gave you this thing, right?" asked Selvi. "Are you sure she loves you?"

"No, actually. So... what do we do now?"

"Good question," said Uncle. He rolled dice and adjusted the placement of pieces on the map. "Gwen and Cassie took out one warrior. Louis's group took out three more. The one Selvi fought has run afoul of that badger on the north end. The bug-eaters are busy with the leader -- who is way above your level before you ask. So these three are your last challenge for the night. Whatcha gonna do? Cynthia, you're up first."

"Um..." Cynthia was leafing through the cards of all her available spells. "I'm gonna use Tangle Grass on the big guy."

A die roll rattled from behind the big divider. "And... wow, critical failure for the bandit," Uncle announced. "Here we go..."

Chapter 6

The Last Hurrah

The oversized bandit yelled in surprise as the grass around his feet suddenly grew long, knotting itself around his ankles. A second later, something large and heavy slammed into his gut, followed by a swift kick up between his legs.

Waving his arms in broad circles didn't help at all as he fell over, squashing the bandit mage with a loud -splat-. Grass sprang up around his wrists, his arms, his chest, holding him flat against the ground -- except for the spot where the mage was poking him in the kidneys. It was only slightly less uncomfortable than the feeling of a sharpened blade being held to his neck.

"Go ahead," growled the most intimidatingly feminine voice he'd ever heard. "Try something." The rough alto seemed to be begging him to give its owner an excuse.

Not far away, a different girl's voice -- a soprano, this time -- shouted "El Kabong!" There was a dull thud and a high-pitched squeal that he barely recognized as his older brother.

The Mistress's voice was still there in his head, but the echoes were fading away quickly. A moment later, and they were gone completely, only to be replaced by shivering fear at the memory of his time with that monster. The young woman now standing with a boot on his chest and a sword at his throat was only slightly less terrifying.

If the bandit had ever been a brave man, his experiences had broken him of that habit. There was a time to stand tall and defiant and a time to blubber like a baby.

So he did.

"Once Louis and Phil's group ganged up on the leader, it released its hold on the bandits," Uncle was saying. "None of them want to fight now. In fact, they'd probably pee themselves if Selvi said 'Boo!' loudly enough."

"Maybe I should," Shelby said approvingly.

"So, to wrap up: the bug-eaters force the leader to make an emergency exit via magic. You all stick around long enough to help them clear out the last of the workers. Louis will take care of the bandits for now since they're victims of the ants as much as anyone, and his group's code requires them to help. You've all got your packs back, slightly singed from Bianca's fire potion but otherwise intact. The ants had a bunch of loot stored up, so you've got a fair bit of gold coming your way, plus some odds and ends that I haven't decided on yet. Most importantly, you've now got a better map of the route south. But..." Uncle pointed towards the door. "I think that will have to wait for another day."

Sometime in the last ten minutes, parents had arrived. Shelby's dad was there, bushy blond beard and all, with a slender, dark-skinned woman by his side who had exactly the same curly hair as her daughter. Mr. McCall was there for Cynthia, along with a skinny-looking guy who was probably Katelyn's dad. Helen's mom was discussing the pizza fees with Max over by the register.

"So, same time next week, ladies?" he asked.

"Yeah!" shouted Helen, Cynthia, and Claire as loud as they could. Katelyn smiled while Shelby managed a "Sure, maybe" before getting up to join her parents.

"Enjoyed yourself after all, huh?" he heard her dad say. "Maybe. Whatever," came the expected response.

"C'mon, Katelyn!" Cynthia said, grabbing the quiet girl by the arm. "We gotta tell our dads how awesome our princesses are!" The two of them were off like a shot.

"Thanks for doing this," said Helen's mom as she came over to claim her daughter. His niece and Claire were busy bagging dice for him.

"Not a prob, sis. They all seemed to enjoy it. Or were you all just faking, ladies?" "It was great!" his niece declared.

"Super-fantastic, Uncle game-dude!"

He had to roll his eyes at that, but he chuckled anyway. "So, Claire. Do you need a ride home?"

"Nah, I live right around the corner. Thanks anyway."

"Will this really be turning into a regular thing?" his sister asked.

"Hope so. Everyone did seem to have fun tonight, so why not? As long as someone's willing to spring for pizza!" He winked. It had been a good evening, for sure, and he did hope that they'd continue. Even the random stuff he'd thrown at the girls had turned out pretty good, and it would be fun to work with it more.

Epilogue

In the highest tower of the Academy, there was a room that Lady Amberyll kept to host little parties. In the center, there was a low table, now heavily laden with treats. Mistress Fresnelding had made several of her favorite recipes, including a thick pie of cheese, meat, and pulped tomato baked in a cast-iron pan. Smaller bowls of fruit lay half-empty around the crumb-filled pan now, and several bottles of wine lay emptier under the table.

"Well," began Mistress Penskill as she deactivated her scrying orb. "That did not go as expected." The gnome tsked and shook her light blue head.

"But it was not a disaster, either," noted Mistress Madonnel, the teacher for the natural philosophies. " I dare say that they acquitted themselves quite well." In the chair next to her, Mistress Mehl of the training salle nodded.

"I am more worried that the Red Queen had a contingent so close to our school," said Lady Amberyll. Her green eyes narrowed. "And to send one of her own lesser daughters with it, no less. We owe Phllthothplp and his band a debt, and not simply for aiding our students in their time of need." The ant-eater's torturous name flowed effortlessly from her lips.

"Those girls had the luck of the clouds and mountains," Mistress Heyerwif pointed out. The half-giant librarian was seated on the floor but still towered over the rest. "They may not, the next time."

"They shall learn, and they shall live," said Amberyll. "And we shall watch. And occasionally laugh. Now," she concluded, raising her glass to the lamplight. "Do we have any more of that Kinbaresi red?"

To be continued in *Princesses of the Pizza Parlor, episode 2: Princesses Never Get Lost*

Thank you for reading. If you liked the story, feel free to leave a few kind words on the website of your choice, and don't forget to follow the author on Twitter, @maikel_yarimizu.

Made in the USA
Middletown, DE
20 November 2021

52694077R00073